THE PUPPY PLACE

BENTLEY

THE PUPPY PLACE

Don't miss any of these other stories by Ellen Miles!

THE PUPPY PLACE

BENTLEY

ELLEN MILES

SCHOLASTIC INC.

Special thanks to Kristin Earhart

Copyright © 2019 by Ellen Miles
Cover art by Tim O'Brien
Original cover design by Steve Scott

ISBN 978-1-338-30302-5

10 9 8 7 6 5 4 3 2 1   19 20 21 22 23

Printed in the U.S.A.   40
First printing 2019

CHAPTER ONE

Charles gazed out the car window down a long valley filled with trees in shades of rosy red, bright yellow, and burnt orange. The grass was still a fresh green, like spring. The colors were beautiful, but Charles couldn't wait for the road to start climbing up into the hills. He couldn't wait to breathe the crisp, mountain air. His puppy, Buddy, was super excited, too. The Petersons were off to the mountains for the weekend!

Was Lizzie excited? Charles wasn't so sure about his older sister. The trip was all because of her, but she was very quiet. She sat on the other side of the backseat, counting on her fingers. Every once in a while, she pulled a carefully folded sheet of paper from the pocket of her purple fleece jacket. Charles knew it was a checklist. Lizzie had been carrying it around for a week, ever since her last Greenies meeting.

Greenies was the name of Lizzie's nature club. Lizzie was in it with her best friend, Maria, and a bunch of older kids from their school. Even though Charles was not a member of the Greenies, he had been invited on the club's big annual camping trip to Misty Valley. Mom and Dad were invited, too!

So was the Bean, Charles's younger brother, but he was staying with Aunt Amanda for the weekend. Charles was sure the Bean was very happy, since Aunt Amanda had a house full of animals. Charles wrapped his arm around Buddy and looked back out the window. He was pretty happy, too. But Lizzie was still looking very serious.

"Why are you so worried?" Charles asked.

"What?" Lizzie said. "Who me? Why do you think I'm worried?"

Charles shrugged. "Because you keep staring at that paper and mumbling to yourself."

"This paper happens to be my checklist," Lizzie explained.

"Yeah, but you already checked everything off, like fifteen times," Charles pointed out.

"I'm just making sure," said Lizzie. "And besides, all the knots I need to know are on the other side. Plus the words to a new camp song."

"I thought camping was supposed to be fun," Charles said.

"It is," Lizzie said. "But remember, the Greenies don't get to stay in cabins like you do. We won't have running water or electricity or beds. We'll get our water from a nearby stream and cook our own food, and put our tents up all by ourselves. The Greenies are doing real camping."

Lizzie sometimes acted like a know-it-all, but Charles knew she had never done camping like this before. He could tell she was nervous.

Charles was glad he was staying in a cabin with Mom and Dad and Buddy. Leave the real camping to Lizzie. Let her tie knots and put up tents and swat bugs. Charles and Buddy were going to have fun!

Buddy had been Charles's best friend ever since he'd come to live with the Petersons. Buddy had started out as a foster puppy—the Petersons had taken care of dozens of puppies who needed homes—but unlike all their other fosters, he had stayed forever and become part of the family. Charles gave the little brown mixed-breed puppy another hug. He was so glad Buddy could come with them on this adventure.

"I think you're really going to enjoy this chal-lenge, Lizzie," Mom said now, from the front seat.

"I think so, too," Dad agreed. "And if you don't

fill up on the canned beans you heat over the fire, we'll steal some real food for you from the mess hall in the lodge."

Dad grinned into the rearview mirror, and Charles laughed. But Lizzie scowled. "Beans *are* real food," she said. "But that's not what we're eating, anyway."

"You can't exist on s'mores all weekend," Dad said. Charles could tell he was still trying to get a smile out of Lizzie.

She crossed her arms. "What's that mean? Do you guys think I can't do this?" Lizzie asked.

"We're not saying that at all," Mom said. She turned around to look into the backseat. She smiled at Lizzie. "It's great that you're taking this on. We're proud of you."

Charles nodded at his older sister. "And it's cool that we can come along."

"Even if you do have to sleep in a cabin," Lizzie said, sounding more like herself. "Maria and I are sharing a two-person tent. We've practiced putting it up. We're a great team."

"I've slept in tents before," said Charles, "with David and Sammy." He could handle real camping as well as Lizzie could, even if she didn't think so.

"Sure," said Lizzie. "In David's backyard, maybe. Not exactly the same thing."

Charles started to reply, but Dad interrupted.

"Look, we're here!" Dad pointed to a sign that said MISTY VALLEY, then turned the car down a long gravel driveway.

"Misty Valley, our home away from home for the weekend," Mom said.

As they got closer, Charles saw small log houses scattered around an open meadow that nestled in among the hills. Charles guessed that those were the sleeping cabins. In the middle of them all were some larger buildings. Dad turned the car toward the one with a sign that read WELCOME CENTER. The building next to it, the largest of all, was made out of stone. It looked like an old castle, with extra tall windows that looked out on a mountain stream. That building had a sign that read MESS HALL. Charles knew that a mess hall was like a cafeteria for campers. He felt his stomach grumble as he wondered what there would be for dinner. Beans 'n' weenies, maybe? Or chili? Maybe there would even be ice cream for dessert.

"There's Maria!" Lizzie said. Her friend sat on a bench in front of the mess hall. Maria looked as calm as always, her long, dark hair straight and shiny. She was surrounded by a mound of sleeping bags, food coolers, and other camping gear. Lizzie leapt out of the car and ran over to Maria.

"Charles, how about if you come with me?" Dad suggested. "You can help me sign in."

Charles climbed out of the car. His legs were stiff as he took the first few steps after that long ride.

A bell jingled when Dad opened the welcome center door. There wasn't anyone at the sign-in counter. "Hello!" Dad called.

There wasn't a person in sight—but the place was not empty. Charles could hear snuffling and scratching. He was almost positive that he recognized those sounds.

Dad started looking through the flyers and papers on the counter, but Charles was feeling curious. He peeked around the tall counter. Sure enough, he saw a metal dog crate—and inside the crate was a sleek gray puppy with long silky ears and slate-blue eyes. The dog tilted his head to look at Charles, staring right back at him. "Dad, look!" said Charles. "It's a puppy!"

CHAPTER TWO

"Hey there. Welcome to Misty Valley." A man with a short gray beard came into the room. His blue plaid shirt, tucked into his corduroy pants, was a little tight over his broad belly. "I'm Melvin Merrick. Sorry to keep you waiting." He smiled as he stuck out his hand to shake Dad's.

"No problem—we just got here," said Dad. "I'm Paul Peterson, and my son, Charles, is—"

"Aha!" the man said as he spotted Charles. "You found Bentley, did you?"

Charles looked up and smiled at Mr. Merrick. "Hi," he said. Then he went back to staring at the pup's silky gray fur.

At home, Lizzie had a "Dog Breeds of the

World" poster. If Charles remembered right, this puppy was probably at least part Weimaraner. His size and color were the main clues. He was tall for a puppy, and he was a beautiful shade of blue gray. Plus, his eyes were blue, with a lot of gray in them.

The only other thing Charles could remember about Weimaraners was that they were intelligent. Charles was sure this dog was smart. He'd seen how the puppy had looked up alertly when the man said his name.

"Hi, Bentley," Charles said, to see if the puppy would react to his name again. Bentley pawed at the crate door. He whined and stared up at Charles with his intense eyes.

Hi, hi, hi! Can we play?

The blankets at the bottom of Bentley's crate were ripped to shreds. Charles felt bad for him.

He knew Bentley must be bored to do that. Puppies needed to be able to roam around and explore their brand-new world.

"How old is Bentley?" Charles asked. He thought the puppy looked like he might be about six months old, but Charles was never as good at telling ages as Lizzie was.

"Your guess is as good as mine." Melvin shrugged as he pushed the sign-in book toward Dad. "Fill in all your information, then sign down at the bottom." He handed Dad a pen. Then he frowned down at Bentley. "He isn't exactly my pup."

"What do you mean?" Charles asked.

"Well, he showed up a couple of weeks ago," Melvin said. "It was a big weekend for camping. We were full, every last cabin and tent site." Melvin gestured at the sign-in book. "I know Bentley must have come then, but no one registered a dog. No one at all. Then everyone packed up and left on Sunday, and the pup was still here."

Charles couldn't believe it. Who would leave such a beautiful dog behind? And why?

"He had a collar on, but no tag. I called all the campers we had that weekend, and no one called back." Melvin clicked his tongue as he shook his head. "Good thing I had this crate left from my son Holling's dog, Bones." He shook his head. "Holling never quite got over losing that old basset hound. He said he'd never get another dog, but somehow I never did get rid of the crate."

Charles smiled. He already liked Melvin—and he *really* liked Bentley.

But Bentley didn't like the crate. The puppy's eyes darted from Charles to Melvin, and back to Charles.

Who's going to let me out? Please let me out. I need to run! I need to play!

Charles scooted on his knees so he could get a closer look at Bentley. The puppy barked with excitement, then pawed at the latch to the crate door.

"Can I let him smell my hand?" Charles asked.

"Sure, he's friendly," Melvin said. "I guess that'll help when we start trying to find him a new home."

Ding, ding, ding! A bell went off in Charles's head. "You're looking for a new home for Bentley?" he asked.

Melvin nodded. "I hate to say it, since I've gotten attached to the little guy, but I think we'll probably need to. We're way too busy here to take care of a puppy."

Charles got it. His family knew all about matching puppies to new families. They had been helping dogs find their forever homes for a while, and they knew each puppy had special needs. *Maybe we can help find Bentley's new family*, Charles thought.

The Petersons were only at Misty Valley for the weekend. He'd have to be quick about it.

"You know," Charles began as Bentley sniffed his hand, "my family brought our puppy to Misty Valley. His name's Buddy. He's very good with other dogs. Maybe we could take Bentley out for you, and they could play together." If Charles could see the dogs together, he'd learn more about Bentley's personality. That was so important when you were finding a new home for a puppy.

"That's nice, but I don't want to trouble you folks. You're here to have fun," Melvin said. He glanced over and smiled as Bentley licked the tips of Charles's fingers.

Watching two puppies play *would* be fun, but Charles didn't want to seem pushy.

"Bentley's a good name," Dad said, his eyes still on the registration he was filling out.

"Yeah, I named him after those fancy British cars," Melvin explained. "The pup has a real sophisticated look about him, all sleek and silver. My son loved those silver Bentleys when he was little, so the name just popped into my head. I think it suits the pup. I bet Holling will agree. He's coming to help out this weekend."

Charles agreed that the puppy was elegant. His coat was so shiny and his legs were so long. Even stuck in the crate, he seemed graceful. Charles wondered about Melvin's son, Holling. What was he like? Charles knew he didn't want another dog and he loved fancy cars. He pictured a guy in a suit who lived in the city and worked at a bank or some other important business place.

Charles tried to push his fingers through the bars on the crate so he could scratch behind Bentley's floppy ears.

Dad pushed the registration book back across the counter. Melvin opened a drawer and pulled out a set of keys. The key chain was a short stick with some rainbow-colored yarn wrapped around it. "You all are in the Wolf Ridge cabin." He handed Dad the keys and pointed toward one of the log houses across the meadow.

"Thanks," Dad replied. "Come on, Charles."

Charles held his hand out to Bentley for one last sniff, and then he got up. "Thanks, Bentley," he said with a wave. "I'll see you soon!" He waved to Melvin, too.

Charles couldn't wait to tell Lizzie all about Bentley. He knew she would have all kinds of advice for him. He rushed out into the brisk air and blinked as his eyes got used to the light.

"Lizzie!" he yelled as he jogged to the car. "Lizzie, there's a Weimaraner puppy in the welcome center. His name is Bentley. He's so cute!" Charles expected Lizzie to race straight into the center, but she was busy rummaging around in the backseat of the car.

"Not now, Charles, I'm running really late," Lizzie said.

"Did you hear me?" Charles asked, poking her.

"I heard you. But I can't find my canteen, and we're supposed to be meeting up with the group. Where is that thing? I had it out for the drive."

"There's a Weimaraner puppy, or at least part-Weimaraner puppy, and he needs a new home," Charles said again. He couldn't even see Lizzie's head. It was almost totally under the seat.

"Lizzie!" Maria called from where all the Greenies were gathered. "Come on. If we don't line up now, they're going to leave without us!"

"Be right there!" Lizzie emerged with a sigh and her canteen. "Weimaraners are awesome," she said as she tucked her canteen into a back-pack pouch. "I wish I could meet him, but it's just going to have to wait."

Then Lizzie couldn't seem to resist showing off how much she knew about dogs. She held up a finger to Maria to signal she'd be there in a second, and let loose with a whole bunch of information, talking double time. "Did you know that Weimaraners' eyes are bright blue until about six months, and then they change to gray or blue gray or amber? Cool, huh?" She ran her hands over her pockets, checking for everything. "And they're super athletic. But they can be tricky. They say that some Weimaraners are smarter than their owners," she added.

"Oh, yes, you're very smart, too," she said, leaning down to pet Buddy, who was pawing at her leg. She gave him a kiss and scratched him behind both ears. Next she gave quick hugs to Mom and Dad before she hurried over to join the Greenies group. She turned around for a second and yelled, "Charles, have fun with Buddy and Bentley!" Then she headed for the hills and her great camping adventure.

CHAPTER THREE

Charles had about a hundred questions for Lizzie, and now she was gone. Lizzie probably knew lots more about Weimaraners, and Charles was eager for more information. He wanted to know more so he could help find Bentley the perfect forever home. He could do it on his own, without Lizzie's help—he knew he could, and he wanted to prove it to her. But it wasn't going to be easy.

As he walked to the cabin with Mom, Dad, and Buddy, Charles went over what he knew. Lizzie had said Weimaraners were smart—sometimes smarter than their owners. Charles wasn't sure what Lizzie meant by that. She also said they were athletic. If they were athletic, he knew that must mean they were also full of energy.

"Do you know anything about Weimaraners?" Charles asked his parents as they headed to their cabin. "Mr. Merrick needs our help finding a new home for Bentley."

"Well, he didn't exactly ask for our help," Dad said.

"But you saw Bentley, Dad," Charles insisted. "That puppy did not want to be in that crate."

"Some dogs don't mind crates," Mom said. "Especially not at night."

"Well, Bentley isn't one of them," said Charles. "He needs a home where he can run around."

"Well, we can talk about this later," Mom said. "For now, let's get settled and look at the schedule of activities for the afternoon."

The cabin was small and cozy, with a bunk bed in the main room for Charles and a small bedroom for Mom and Dad. Charles tossed his backpack on top of the red wool blanket covering the bottom bunk.

"This is nice," said Mom, looking around. "I like the red plaid curtains. Very quaint." She sat down next to Charles and showed him the brochure Dad had taken at the welcome center. "There's a birdwatching hike on Sunday." She ran a finger down the schedule. "This afternoon, you have two choices," she said. "Flying Squirrel or the Raptor Shack. Flying Squirrel sounds exciting—you fly high above the trees. And at the Raptor Shack you can see the injured birds the rangers are taking care of—big birds! Hawks and owls."

Charles wasn't so sure about Flying Squirrel, but the Raptor Shack sounded cool.

"It'd be neat to see some of the big birds that live around here," Dad said. "But we probably couldn't take Buddy. He might bark. He could scare them."

"Or they might want to eat him," Mom added.

Charles stared at Mom, horrified.

Mom laughed. "Just kidding. But a raptor is a bird of prey by definition," Mom said. "And Buddy is still pretty small."

"I'll do Flying Squirrel," Charles said quickly. "So Buddy can come."

"We'd better hurry," Dad said. "They're starting now. I'll come with you, so I can hold Buddy while you're being a squirrel. I just hope he doesn't want to chase you the way he wants to chase the squirrels in our backyard!"

As they crossed the meadow behind their cabin, Charles spotted a kid already way up high, swinging from a tree branch. She was held up by a harness that went around her waist and legs. Charles gulped as he watched her hold out her arms and pretend to fly. "Wheee!" she cried.

Buddy saw the girl, too. He started barking. "It's all right, Buddy," Charles said, but he was really trying to reassure himself.

When Charles joined the kids waiting in line, a young woman came up to him. "Hey, I'm Shawna," she said with a big smile. "Welcome to Flying Squirrel."

"This is Charles," Dad said.

"And this is Buddy," Charles added.

"Aw, Buddy. What a cutie. Can I pet him?" While Shawna scratched Buddy behind his ears, she told Charles all about the activity. "You don't have to go that high," Shawna said, motioning to the boy who had been next in line. "You just tell me when you're ready to fly. Or yell out to the people holding the rope that pulls you up." She pointed to a group of young men and women wearing fleece jackets with the green Misty Valley logo on the backs. "They can move you higher or lower, whatever you want."

Charles nodded, but he couldn't take his eyes off the boy in the harness. He had stretched his arms into a V like a superhero. "Check it out!" he yelled as he soared through the air.

"You know what I can't wait to see?" Shawna said, sounding excited. "I can't wait to see Buddy's reaction when it's your turn."

The line moved quickly. It wasn't long before it was Charles's turn to put on the gear. Buddy watched as Charles stepped into the harness. The puppy sniffed the tightly woven red fabric and whimpered a little. When it was time for Charles to follow Shawna into the clearing, Dad had to hold Buddy back.

Shawna hooked Charles's safety harness to the rope with a steel clasp called a carabiner. "Give a thumbs-up when you're ready," Shawna directed. Charles nodded. He stood in the middle of the clearing for a moment, taking a few deep breaths. Then he pressed his lips together, closed his eyes, and raised his thumb. Almost immediately, he could feel the pull on the harness. Then, just like that, he was up in the air. He hung there, getting the feel of it, until Shawna called out to him.

"All good?" she yelled. "Thumbs-up?"

Charles didn't even think about it. He put his thumb way up. Then he raised his other hand and spread both arms way out. The rangers with the rope took several steps back, lifting him higher.

Charles swung back and forth, far above everyone—including Dad and Buddy. He was flying! Far below, Dad waved. He looked just like Dad—only smaller. Charles saw that Shawna had walked over to Dad and Buddy. She bent down and was talking to Buddy, pointing up to Charles. Charles saw how Buddy watched with his ears alert, but he didn't hear his puppy bark.

It was all over way too soon, and Charles rushed to get back in line for another turn. After his second flight, Dad said it was time to meet Mom for dinner. Shawna headed over when she saw them leaving. "You were awesome, Charles!" she said.

"Thanks," he said. "It was really fun."

"Buddy was super impressed. I could tell." Shawna stroked Buddy's ears.

"What did you say to him when I was up there?" Charles asked. "What did you say so he didn't bark?"

"Oh, that's our little secret," she answered, smiling at Buddy. "Isn't it, boy?" Buddy looked up at her with his big, sincere brown eyes. "Well, okay, I'll tell him." Shawna nodded and looked back to Charles. "I promised him you would be all right. That's why he didn't bark." Shawna ruffled Buddy's ears as a good-bye. "Have a great night!" she said as she returned to help the other "flyers." Charles smiled and waved to Shawna. She had been so nice to him, and she had a special way with dogs, too.

Charles had a feeling he *would* have a great night—now that he had the perfect home in mind for Bentley.

CHAPTER FOUR

The next morning, Charles woke up just as the first rays of sun found their way through the window by his bunk. Buddy was nuzzling his cold nose against Charles's face.

Charles tried to squirm away, hiding his face in the pillow, but the puppy started to lick his ear. Charles giggled and sat up in bed, pulling Buddy into a hug. It was probably time to get up, anyway, since they were going on an early-morning tree-identification hike.

When he looked up, he saw Mom already fully dressed. Dad was still asleep.

Mom took Buddy outside while Charles got dressed. When Charles was ready, she brought

Buddy back in to leave him with Dad. Dogs were not allowed in the mess hall.

Everything seemed still as they headed down the gravel path. Their breath lingered in the air like fog. As they got closer, they saw campers of all ages walking out of their cabins and heading for the big building.

Breakfast was amazing. Charles wondered what Lizzie was eating but he didn't spend too much time worrying about it. He helped himself to pancakes with real maple syrup, scrambled eggs with ketchup, two sausage links, and chunks of juicy melon. Mom stuck to a healthy breakfast of yogurt and granola with banana—but Charles noticed that she kept sneaking bites from his plate.

Charles had seen other campers on their phones, and he figured out that there was Wi-Fi in the mess hall. Since yesterday, he had been thinking of a list of questions about the Weimaraner breed. When Mom went to get another cup of coffee, she loaned Charles her phone. He quickly found a lot of information about Weimaraners. He was not surprised that everything Lizzie had rattled off was true, but the phone gave him even more details. Wait until he told her everything he'd learned! She would have to be impressed.

For example, Charles found out that the Weimaraner breed started in Germany, and that their original breeders used them as hunting dogs. Just as he'd guessed, Weimaraners were high-energy dogs with a lot of endurance—which meant they needed lots of exercise. He also learned that breeders wanted dogs that were loyal, so Weimaraners were very attached to their people. Charles nodded when he read that. That would probably make Bentley a great family dog.

The most interesting thing Charles read was about their intelligence. Lizzie had said that Weimaraners were sometimes smarter than their owners. Now Charles understood what she meant.

He read some funny stories about Weimaraners who figured out how to unlock gates, or who made their way into a cupboard to steal extra snacks. "A bored Weimaraner is a dangerous thing!" one owner had posted, along with a picture of an open dog-food bin with a silver-gray dog dozing next to it. Charles laughed.

Mom came back to the table, cradling her coffee mug. Charles could see the steam rising from the top. "Find out anything good?" Mom asked.

Charles showed her the picture, and she laughed.

"The more I read, the more I think Bentley should definitely not be stuck in a crate all day," Charles told her. "Weimaraners need exercise, and they want to spend time with their people."

"Well, the first step will be to make sure Mr. Merrick needs our help," Mom said. "We should make sure he really wants to find a new home for Bentley before we go any further."

Charles nodded. Mom was right, as usual. Maybe he was getting a little ahead of himself.

"Come on," Mom said. "Our hike starts soon. We should grab some breakfast for your dad. He's meeting us with Buddy."

Charles would have liked to stay and do more research, but that would have to wait. Anyway, after all that reading about dogs, he wanted to see his own little brown puppy.

The tree-identification hike started at the flagpole, which was on the other side of the camp, close to the Flying Squirrel location. Dad ate his muffin and sipped from a cup of coffee as they walked. Buddy trotted along next to Charles, sniffing at the morning air.

As the Petersons neared the welcome center,

Charles could hear Bentley barking. It was as if the puppy knew a playmate was close by.

"Can Buddy and I go ahead? I could take him to meet Bentley," Charles told his parents.

"I'm not sure that's a good idea, Charles," Mom said. "We don't have a lot of time."

"And I think it would be better for the dogs to meet each other outside," Dad added. "Then they can be on common ground."

Charles thought about what Dad said. He was right. But as they walked closer to the welcome center, Bentley started barking even louder. Charles really wished the silver puppy could get outside more.

Just then, the door of the center flew open. Bentley appeared, tail wagging like a thick whip. Behind him stood Mr. Merrick, holding the puppy's leash.

Buddy rushed ahead, pulling his leash tight.

Bentley's tail went up, and his ears went on alert. He stared at Buddy with his intense blue eyes and grinned a doggy grin.

A friend! At last! I am so happy that another puppy is here. I need to get closer. Now! Hurry up. He's right there!

Buddy pulled on the leash, yanking Charles along. Bentley dragged Mr. Merrick toward Buddy. It was obvious that both puppies had one thing in mind: they were ready to play!

"Good morning, Mr. Merrick!" Charles said as soon as the two puppies had reached each other. They sniffed and snuffled and pawed at each other happily.

"Morning, Charles," the camp director said. "This must be your puppy." He smiled down at Buddy. "Aren't you a nice-looking dog?" he said as he struggled to keep the leashes from getting tangled.

"Yes, this is Buddy," said Charles. "I've told him all about Bentley."

Bentley towered over Buddy. Buddy hunched down with his front paws stretched out and his hind end in the air, doing what Lizzie called a "play bow," when one dog invited another to play. Bentley sniffed him all over and then barked.

Absolutely! Let's play!

Buddy playfully nipped at the air, and Bentley jumped up on his hind legs, waving his front paws at Buddy.

With his oversized ears, extra-wide paws, and gangly legs, Bentley was clearly a puppy. Still, he was tall! Charles could tell he was going to grow to be a sleek, elegant dog.

"Bentley, no," said Mr. Merrick. "You're too big

to pounce on Buddy that way." He knelt down to give the puppy long, reassuring strokes. "I'm sorry," he said to Charles. "I don't think he's been around other dogs much yet."

"It's okay," Charles replied, but he was relieved that Mr. Merrick had stepped in. Bentley *was* a lot bigger than Buddy, and he might not know how to play nicely with other dogs.

Just then, there was the sound of car wheels on the gravel driveway. An SUV had pulled into the welcome center parking lot. "New arrivals," Mr. Merrick said. "Bentley, we've got to go in." But when Mr. Merrick tugged on his leash, Bentley began to whine and pull back.

Buddy whined, too. Charles felt bad for both puppies. They had just started to get to know each other. "Come on, Buddy," he said, pulling gently on his puppy's leash. "Time for our hike. We'll see Bentley later."

But Buddy would not budge.

CHAPTER FIVE

Charles held Buddy's leash tight as the puppy strained to get closer to Bentley.

Bentley was sticking firm to his spot, all four feet planted to the ground.

Don't make me go back in there! It's so much more fun being outside with my new friend.

"I know, boy," Mr. Merrick said, "but I've got a job to do." He started toward the welcome center, but Bentley didn't follow. His whining was louder.

Charles tried again to pull Buddy away. He didn't want to make it harder for Bentley to leave. Buddy pulled back, toward Bentley.

"How about we take Bentley on the nature hike with us?" Dad said to Mr. Merrick. "He could get some more fresh air, and Buddy would like the company."

Charles's eyes lit up. "Yeah! It would be great for both puppies."

"Oh, no," said Mr. Merrick. "I don't want to trouble you."

"It's no trouble at all," Mom assured him.

Mr. Merrick looked over to where a family was piling out of the SUV. Then he looked down at Bentley. Bentley stared up at Mr. Merrick, his forehead wrinkled and his head cocked. He held up one paw.

Please, please, please. I want to stay outside and get to know my new friend. Please, please, please.

"Oh, okay," said Mr. Merrick, shaking his head and laughing. "How can I resist that face? He does tug pretty hard on the leash, so I think it's better if one of the adults holds him." He knelt down to put his large hands on either side of Bentley's head. "These nice folks are going to take good care of you. I'll see you soon."

Charles grinned as they headed off together. This was going to be the most fun hike ever! He couldn't wait to see the two puppies explore and play together.

While they all waited at the flagpole, the young dogs did just that. There was a lot of sniffing and pawing, and a few happy barks as the puppies wrestled. Charles could have watched them all day, but after a few moments the ranger showed up and said it was time to go.

Once the hike started, the puppies were less interested in each other and more interested in the ground, the rocks, and the trees. They smelled *everything*. Charles held Buddy, and Dad took Bentley's leash. The Petersons had to work to keep up with the rest of the group.

It had rained overnight, and the forest floor was still wet. "Watch out for moss on rocks," the ranger called back to the group. "Moss can be slippery on mornings like this."

The ranger, who had introduced himself as Logan, seemed to know everything about the forest. He showed them how maple leaves had five points, explained that the leaves of beech trees turn a bright lemon yellow in the fall, and pointed out acorns that had dropped from oak trees.

When Logan showed them a tree with a red-tailed hawk's nest high in the branches, Mom pulled out her binoculars. "Are you leading the birdwatching walk tomorrow?" she asked.

"Yep, bright and early," Logan replied.

Just then, they all heard the sound of voices floating up from the other side of a hill. Charles thought it sounded like one of the songs Lizzie had been practicing. Buddy's ears pricked up, and he lifted his nose. "What is it, boy?" Charles asked.

Before Buddy could even bark, a group of Greenies appeared at the top of the hill. Charles could see Lizzie and Maria near the front of the pack, hand in hand. As soon as Lizzie saw them, she ran down the hill.

"Buddy!" she cried, kneeling down so the puppy could jump into her lap. "How are you, boy? Are you going to introduce me to your friend?"

Bentley whined and tugged on his leash so he could get close to Lizzie, too. He stared at her with his intense blue-gray eyes until she reached out to pet him.

Yes! I love a scratch behind the ears almost as much as I love being outside. This is the best morning!

"Charles told me you were a cutie," Lizzie cooed to Bentley. She stroked his long silky ears. She giggled as he licked her face. Lizzie cuddled both puppies as she told her family all about her camping trip so far. "We've been hiking, and wading in the creek, and eating such great food," she said. "You wouldn't believe what you can cook over a wood campfire!"

Charles rolled his eyes. Lizzie thought she was so cool because she was camping. He'd cooked hot dogs and marshmallows over a fire plenty of times—what was the big deal?

"Lizzie, we better catch up," Maria interrupted, motioning to the rest of the Greenies. The group was heading down a different path.

"Gotta go," Lizzie said, giving both puppies a final kiss. Then she and Maria ran after the other campers. When she reached the top of another hill, she turned around. "I remembered one more thing about Weimaraners," she yelled to Charles. "They're related to bloodhounds! They have an amazing sense of smell!"

"Thanks!" Charles yelled back. He had to hand

it to her: Lizzie did know a lot about dogs. He turned to look for Logan and saw that the rest of the group was far down the trail. Charles and his parents hurried along. As soon as they neared the rest of the hikers, Charles realized something was wrong. Everyone stood in a circle, staring down at a little boy who sat on the ground, holding his foot as tears streaked down his face.

"What happened?" Dad asked one of the hikers, a woman in a plaid shirt.

"We were crossing the stream, and this boy slipped on a rock," she said pointing to the boy. "Slippery moss, just like Logan said."

Logan examined the boy's foot. "Does this hurt?" he asked as he touched it gently.

Bentley pulled the leash out of Dad's hands and bounded up to the boy. He pushed his nose up against the boy's cheek and wagged his tail, whimpering.

Are you okay? It'll all be fine. Don't worry. Don't even think about your foot. Pet me instead! Pet me! Pet me!

"Bentley!" Dad said.

But the ranger smiled at the silver pup. "You can pet him, Mateo," Logan said to the boy. "Just let me have a look at that foot." Logan pressed the boy's ankle again, and the boy flinched a little. But now Mateo was much more interested in Bentley than his injury. When they were done, Logan gave Bentley's ears a rub. "That's a good boy, Bentley. Thanks for the distraction, little guy."

Charles noticed how good Bentley was with Mateo. The puppy licked the little boy's face gently and sat calmly as Mateo petted him.

Charles noticed something else, too. He noticed how good Logan was with Bentley. If things didn't work out with Shawna, maybe there was still hope for finding the pup a great home.

CHAPTER SIX

"After that hike I'm ready for a nap," Dad said after lunch.

"And I want to read my bird book," said Mom.

"I still want to play capture the flag," said Charles. Camp was so much fun! "Can Bentley and Buddy stay with you?"

"Of course," said Mom. "They'll entertain each other, I'm sure." Dad had checked with Mr. Merrick to see if Bentley could stay with them until dinnertime since the two puppies were having such a good time together.

Charles thought the puppies might need a nap, too. They'd had so much exercise that morning, running up and down the trail. By the end of the hike, Buddy had been slowing down. Finally, he just sat—right in the middle of the trail. That was the sign that he was tired and wanted someone to pick him up. Dad had carried Buddy for the last part of the hike. Even Bentley was panting by the time they got back to the flagpole.

Charles liked capture the flag. He'd played it lots of times at school. He was always good at coming up with a strategy. Now, at Misty Valley, he was extra happy when he saw that Shawna was the referee for the game. Charles volunteered to guard his team's jail. He hoped that would put him in position to talk to Shawna a little more. After all, his family was only there for the weekend. He didn't have much time if he was going to find Bentley a new home.

Of course, he also had to keep his eye on his team's hidden flag.

Remembering what Logan had taught them during the morning's hike, he'd suggested they hide their bright yellow flag in the yellow leaves of a beech tree. Now he could barely see the flag from where he stood, so he knew his idea had been a good one.

While Charles's team hid their yellow flag, the other team needed to hide and protect a red one. He peered across the meadow, trying to see where they'd put it.

"I see Buddy has met Bentley," Shawna said to Charles once the game started. She pointed to a picnic table on the sidelines.

Charles glanced over to see that Dad had come out to watch the game, with both dogs. He must have given up on his nap. The puppies were rolling in the grass. Every time they collided, they nipped and wrestled in a friendly way. Charles smiled. So Shawna already knew Bentley. That was a good sign.

"Yeah," Charles replied, watching the action in the game at the other end of the field. "Bentley is awesome. He's such a fun puppy. He's really energetic, happy, and smart." He watched Shawna's face to see her reaction. He could tell she agreed with him about Bentley, just by the way she smiled as she watched the dogs play.

"All Weimaraners are smart," he added, "but I think Bentley is super smart." Charles realized that he sounded a lot like Lizzie. She was always going on and on about dogs. But he couldn't stop himself. He needed to make his point. He needed to convince Shawna to adopt Bentley.

Just as Charles was about to add that the breed was extremely loyal, Shawna spoke up. "I know," she said, her eyes still on the capture-the-flag action. "Mr. Merrick told me he wants to find Bentley a new home. I'd love to adopt him, but I already have three full-grown dogs in a small apartment. I think Bentley needs a lot of attention, and my guys demand all my time."

Charles's heart rose when he heard for sure

that Mr. Merrick wanted to find Bentley a new home. But then he realized what else Shawna had said: that she couldn't adopt Bentley. His heart sank way back down to his tummy. It felt worse than the moment he thought he was falling during the Flying Squirrel. He had convinced himself that Shawna was perfect for Bentley.

"Uh-oh, Charles," Shawna said. "Looks like you're going to be busy. Some kids on Team Red are headed for jail."

Shawna was right—about the game, but especially about Bentley. Charles knew that the silver pup did need someone who could give him lots of love and attention. Charles still wanted to find that person, but time was running out. If Shawna wasn't going to adopt Bentley, maybe it was time to start thinking about whether Logan would.

Later, Charles couldn't even remember how the rest of the game had gone. He was in a hurry for it to be over. He wanted to concentrate on Bentley.

When they took Bentley back to the welcome center, Charles was ready. He took Bentley in while Dad and Buddy waited outside. "Hey, Mr. Merrick," he said. "Thanks for letting us keep Bentley for the day."

"Sure thing," the camp director said, coming out from behind the counter. He knelt down to greet the puppy.

"Bentley really liked that hike with Logan. Logan liked Bentley, too. He said Bentley was extra helpful when he helped a hurt kid feel better." Charles took a deep breath as he watched the older man's face.

"Did you do that, boy?" Mr. Merrick asked, rubbing the puppy all over. Bentley ran in a tight circle in front of the camp director, then jumped up on his knees, panting in his face.

Today was so fun! So, so, so fun! But I missed you. It's good to see you again, too!

"Logan was really great with Bentley," Charles said. "He seems like a nice guy. Do you know if he has any dogs?"

"I don't think Logan has a dog right now," said Mr. Merrick. "But you're right—he's really nice. He and my son used to work together. They'd go up north to the ski resorts in the winter. They had a lot of fun. I think Logan will be heading up there soon."

Charles nodded. This was good. Mr. Merrick liked Logan. That was important.

After dinner, Charles and his parents headed to the camp bonfire. Everyone at Misty Valley was invited. Charles waved when he spotted Lizzie sitting on a stump by the big, roaring fire. He was surprised to realize how much he had missed her. He couldn't wait to tell her how things were going with finding Bentley a new home. Plus, if they talked about Bentley, at least he wouldn't have to hear more about her fantastic camping skills. He went to sit next to her and told her what Shawna had said about why she couldn't adopt Bentley.

"She's right," Lizzie said. "Bentley will need a lot of attention, so she's not the right match."

"And then I met Logan," Charles said. "He's so great. He was really good with Bentley. He loves to hike, and his winter job is at a ski resort."

"Ski resort?" Lizzie asked.

"Yup! Perfect, right?" Charles said. "Plenty of outside time."

"I don't know." Lizzie shook her head. "Weimaraners have such short hair. They don't like cold weather. I heard they can be kind of wimpy that way."

Charles frowned. Why did she have to say that? Logan was his best candidate for Bentley's new forever owner. Lizzie might know a lot about dogs, but she didn't know Bentley like he did. Charles was sure Bentley could handle a little cold weather.

Charles looked across the bonfire and saw that Mr. Merrick was sitting on a log next to the flames. Bentley sat close beside him, practically on his lap. Charles elbowed Lizzie and pointed the pair out to her.

Lizzie glanced over and smiled. It was a sweet moment. Mr. Merrick stroked Bentley's back while two little girls held their hands out for Bentley to sniff. Bentley sniffed, then licked their fingers all over. Both girls giggled.

Hi, hi, hi! Let's be friends now. I'll give you lots of kisses, so you know I like you.

"Mr. Merrick likes Logan," Charles said. He couldn't let it go. "Logan used to work with his son." Charles watched Mr. Merrick stroke the puppy's head. He could tell he cared a lot about Bentley.

"Mr. Merrick has a son?" Lizzie asked. "What about him? Maybe he can adopt Bentley."

Charles sighed. "Nope. His dog, Bones, died a while ago, and he isn't over it yet. He doesn't want another dog. Mr. Merrick says he still misses that basset hound."

"Hmmm," Lizzie said with a sigh. "Well, Bentley obviously likes kids. Maybe you should think about looking for a family who would like to adopt him."

"We leave tomorrow," Charles reminded Lizzie.

"I don't know how you'll find Bentley an owner by then. But I do know I want a s'more. Come on." Lizzie grabbed Charles by the hand and dragged him over to the s'more station. Charles let himself be dragged. He was still thinking about Bentley, but he could think about chocolate and marsh-mallows, too.

CHAPTER SEVEN

"Blueberry muffins," Mom announced the next morning. Charles rolled over in his bunk and looked toward the door. Mom had just come into the cabin, bringing a blast of brisk air. She carried a plate piled with baked goods and apples. She already had her backpack on, and Charles could see her tall, green, to-go coffee mug in the drink holder on one side. He guessed Dad's red one was in the other.

"Coffee," Dad mumbled from the bedroom.

Charles watched as Dad stumbled out of the room, pulling on his sweater. Now he remembered: they were going on the early bird-watching hike.

Charles sat up. It was their last day at Misty

Valley and he still had so much to do. Only one more day to find Bentley a new home!

He pulled on his clothes and then snapped Buddy's leash onto the puppy's collar. "Can Buddy and I go ahead?" Charles asked. "I want to find out if we can take Bentley birdwatching with us."

"Hold on there, bud," said Dad. "We should all go together, since one of us will have to hold Bentley if Mr. Merrick says yes."

Charles shifted from foot to foot while Dad finished putting on his hiking boots. He was relieved when Mom said they could eat their muffins on the way.

When they left the cabin, Charles understood why the camp was called Misty Valley. A layer of thick, wet fog hovered just above the ground. It filled the meadow where they had played capture the flag. It hung in the cluster of trees where they had flown like squirrels. It was especially thick over the creek that ran down from the hills.

As they walked, Mom began listing birds she hoped they might see on their walk. She ticked them off on her fingers. "Definitely lots of ducks and geese, by the pond. Sharp-shinned hawks. A peregrine falcon. Merlins."

"Merlins?" Charles asked.

"Small falcons," Mom told him. "They can fly really fast, though not as fast as peregrine falcons. Those are one of the fastest birds."

"Why are there so many birds around here?" Charles asked.

"Well, partly because we're in the woods," Mom said. "But also, it's the start of the fall migration and a lot of birds are passing through on their way to warmer spots for the winter."

When they were almost to the welcome center, Charles's parents let him run ahead. Mom held on to Buddy, who tried to chase after Charles.

Charles gave the door a light knock and turned the knob. "Hi, Mr. Merrick," he said. "Can we take Bentley on our hike?"

Mr. Merrick raised a hand and pointed to the phone he held to his ear. "Oops, sorry," said Charles. He had not meant to interrupt.

Charles lingered by the door for a few moments. He inched his way to the side so he could get a glimpse of the Weimaraner puppy. Bentley spotted Charles right away. He wagged his tail so hard it banged against the side of the crate, then let out a little bark.

Hi! You came back! Can we go outside? I want to go with you! I want to play with my friend!

Charles caught Mr. Merrick's eye and motioned toward Bentley, raising his eyebrows. Mr. Merrick covered the end of his phone and shook his head.

"Sorry, Charles," he said. "There's just too much going on today."

Charles nodded to Mr. Merrick. He was disappointed. He had really wanted Bentley to come with them. He knew Buddy would have liked that, too. As soon as he turned toward the door, Charles could hear Bentley whine. Charles tried to tiptoe out, but it was too late. Bentley barked again, a little more loudly this time.

Hey, wait! Don't go yet! Please let me out of this crate!

As Charles slipped out the door and rejoined his parents, Bentley's yips and whines grew louder and longer. Charles could hear the puppy halfway across the campground.

During the walk over to the flagpole, Charles tried to tune out the barking and think about

58

what to say to Logan. What was the best way to convince him to adopt Bentley?

When they joined the others waiting for the hike, Logan waved to them. Then he started to head their way. Charles felt a rush of hope. Maybe Logan had heard Bentley barking. Maybe he was coming over to tell them that he wanted to adopt him.

"I'm sorry," Logan said when he was a few steps away, "but you can't bring your pup on this hike. He might scare away the birds."

Charles had to switch gears quickly. He'd been so sure Logan was going to talk to them about adopting Bentley. "But what will Buddy do?" he asked after a moment. "If we're all on the hike?"

"I'll take him," Dad said. "It's Mom who has really been looking forward to the birdwatching."

Another ranger who had been standing close by spoke up. "I can take you and your dog on a different hike," the older man offered. He pointed

59

past the creek. "Those hills have a good trail. Lots of fall color. And there's a waterfall at the top of the path."

"Thanks," Dad said. He took one last long gulp of coffee from his to-go mug and stuck it back into Mom's backpack pocket. "That sounds great. Charles, you want to come with Buddy and me?"

Charles looked from Mom to Dad. Yes, he wanted to go with Dad and Buddy. The hike yesterday with Buddy—and Bentley—had been so much fun. But he also wanted to go with Mom. Mom had been looking forward to the bird hike all weekend, and she'd probably like to have him along. Plus, Charles really wanted to talk to Logan about Bentley. He wasn't sure if he would get another chance. "I'll go with Mom," Charles said.

Mom smiled and gave one of his shoulders a squeeze. "Great. I'll let you borrow my binoculars," she said.

"Thanks, Bruce," Logan said to the other ranger.

"Sure thing," Bruce replied, giving him a friendly nod. "I love the Boulder Lane Trail this time of year."

"Yeah," Logan agreed. "Just take it easy. There's been a lot of rain."

"Got it," Bruce said, nodding again.

Charles gave Buddy a quick pat, said good-bye to Dad, and headed off with Mom and the rest of the group. "We'll meet back here at the flagpole," Dad called out. Charles gave a thumbs-up and waved.

CHAPTER EIGHT

Birdwatching was a lot harder than Charles had thought it would be, even though Logan was full of tips. He said they should be silent and stay alert. It was a lot like being a spy, except without the black clothes and cool gadgets.

Mom seemed to catch on quickly. When Logan pointed to something in a tree, she would raise the binoculars to her eyes. "Aw," she'd say, or "So pretty." Then she'd pass the binoculars to Charles. He would lift them to his eyes and squint through the eyepieces just in time to catch the flutter of wings as the bird flew away. Still, he was happy to be with Mom.

He learned a lot about raptors. Logan told them

that "raptor" came from a word that meant "to grab or seize," which was how raptors caught their prey. Hawks, falcons, vultures, and owls were all raptors, with fearsome hooked beaks and sharp talons on their feet, which made them good hunters. According to Logan, they ate everything: other birds, frogs and snakes, and small mammals like mice. Logan didn't mention puppies, and Charles didn't ask. He didn't even want to think about a raptor scooping up Buddy.

After they had hiked for about half an hour, the group reached a small clearing. "Let's stop here for a bit and you can look for nests," Logan suggested. "Most birds are done with raising their young by this time of year, but it's a great time to find empty nests in trees and shrubs."

Charles knew this was his chance to talk to the ranger. "I'm going to ask Logan about Bentley," he said to Mom.

Mom lowered the binoculars from her eyes.

"You sure are determined," she said. "Remember, we're not exactly fostering that puppy. He's not our responsibility."

"I know," said Charles. "But Bentley needs a good home. I want to help him."

"I know you do," Mom said. She smiled at him and gave him a little shove toward Logan. "Go ahead."

Charles approached Logan, who was sitting on a log, looking up at the sky.

"Hey," Charles said.

"Hey," Logan replied. He patted a mossy spot on the log next to him.

Charles sat down. He tried to think of a clever way to bring up the topic. He couldn't, so he decided to just dive straight in. "So, you know the puppy that someone left here? At Misty Valley?"

"Sure," Logan said. "You mean Bentley, right? The pup who came along on our hike yesterday?"

"Uh-huh," Charles answered, staring down at

his hands. They were a little red from the cold. "Well, I'm trying to find Bentley a good forever home so he doesn't have to stay in a crate in the welcome center all day." He looked up at Logan's face. Logan's beard was dark brown, and his blue eyes were kind. "You were really good with him yesterday, and I know he'd love to go with you on hikes and stuff."

"Wow, it's so nice of you to think of me. I love dogs and I think Bentley is great," Logan said. "But I have a winter job in the mountains. It keeps me busy all day. I wouldn't have enough time at home to take good care of a puppy."

"Oh," Charles said. "Okay." Now what? He had really been hoping that Logan would say yes. This was strike two, after Shawna had said no. He didn't have much time to find someone else.

"Bentley's such a good dog. I'm sure he'll find a great home with someone, or lots of people, who will love him," Logan said. He sat there quietly with Charles for a moment longer. Then he patted him on the knee and stood up. "I gotta get these folks moving again. I really want them to see a hawk. Maybe a sharp-shinned hawk. They're migrating from Canada about now."

Charles nodded, his eyes on the ground. "My mom would love that," he said. Just then, he didn't care that much about sharp-shinned hawks, or any birds at all. He went back to find Mom. When she saw his face, she let go of the binoculars and let them dangle around her neck. Charles didn't have to say a word; she knew exactly what he was feeling. She gave him a hug. When he pulled away, she kept a hand on his shoulder. They walked that way for a while.

Charles thought about what Logan had said. The ranger had a good point. Bentley did need someone around most of the time. It would be even better if he had lots of people around, lots of people to love him.

Maybe what Bentley needed most was a family. After all, Bentley loved kids. He had comforted Mateo when he fell. He had played with the girls at the bonfire. Even if Charles couldn't be the one to find Bentley a forever home, now he could tell Mr. Merrick what kind of home would be best for the silver pup.

By the time the group was leaving the woods, Charles felt better. He knew he would be able to help Bentley, even if just a little.

"Look! A merlin!" Logan called out just as they came into the meadow. He pointed. "See it, flying past the flagpole? You can tell it from other falcons because it beats its wings faster, and it's usually on the smaller side."

The group stopped, everyone squinting to see the bird against the dull gray sky. Charles looked up, too. He saw the bird, flying fast over the meadow. Then he looked back down to see Bruce, the older ranger, standing by the flagpole.

Charles recognized the wide brim of his felt hat. But Bruce was alone. Dad and Buddy were not with him.

Something was wrong. Where was Dad?

"Mom," said Charles. He tugged on her sleeve. "Mom." His mother was still trying to find the merlin through her binoculars.

Charles stepped away from the group. He raised both hands and waved them. Bruce waved back. Then he motioned to Charles with one hand. "Mom, it's Bruce," Charles said. "He wants us. We have to go to the flagpole." Bruce motioned again, and Charles took off running.

He heard Mom call to him, but he didn't stop. He ran the whole way, nearly stumbling up to Bruce. "What's wrong?" he asked. "Where's my dad?"

"He's fine," Bruce said quickly. "But Buddy got loose, and your dad is trying to track him down."

"What? Loose? Where?" Charles felt his heart thudding in his chest.

"In the woods. Buddy heard something and took off," Bruce explained. "He couldn't have gotten far, but your dad asked me to come back and tell you."

Charles gazed at the hills where Dad and Buddy had gone. The woods went on forever, as far as he could see. What if Buddy got lost in that endless forest? They'd never find him. He glanced back at Mom. She was jogging toward them, the binoculars banging against her chest.

"Hurry!" he yelled to her. "We have to find Buddy!" He took off running, toward the hills.

"Charles, wait!" called Mom.

But Charles didn't stop. Buddy needed his help.

CHAPTER NINE

"Hold on, Charles! I can take you right to your dad," Bruce shouted.

Charles glanced back. Bruce and his mom were running, too. They were right behind him.

Charles forced himself to slow down, but his mind was still racing. What had happened? Buddy liked to be outside, but he liked to be with his people even more. What could have made him disappear?

Charles's mind buzzed with all that Logan had told them about raptors. Maybe a small merlin wouldn't go after a puppy, but Logan had said that owls sometimes hunted larger prey. Charles reminded himself that Logan said owls were nocturnal—they hunted at night. How many hours did they have before sunset?

Charles knew one thing for sure: if he'd been along on the hike with Dad and Bruce, Buddy would never have run off. When Mom reached him, he blurted out, "It's my fault. If I had gone with Dad, Buddy wouldn't have gotten loose."

"Oh, no," Mom said, hugging Charles close. "It's not your fault at all. It isn't anyone's fault. Don't worry. We just need to focus on finding him." She gave him one last squeeze and let him go. "Come on," she said. She grabbed his hand, and they took off up the trail.

"There was a group of hikers," Bruce called out from behind. "They were on a trail up the hill. They were singing. Your dad thinks Buddy might have heard that."

"It must have been the Greenies!" said Charles. "I bet Buddy heard Lizzie and ran off to find her."

It wasn't long before they found Dad. He was striding along the trail, calling Buddy's name. "He went that way," Dad said, pointing. "He still has his leash on."

"I sent out an alert on my walkie-talkie. We'll hear back if anyone finds him," Bruce said. "We should probably head on up the trail and keep our eyes peeled."

Charles scanned the forest floor as they hiked. They were on a dirt path, but he thought he heard a rustle in the dried leaves. Then he was sure he heard a bark. "Quiet!" he declared. "I hear something." The adults all froze in place. Charles crossed his fingers. Was it Buddy?

Charles felt a rush of relief when he saw a pair of floppy ears appear. But then he realized that those ears did not belong to his puppy. Those ears were silver, not brown.

"Bentley? What are you doing here?" Charles asked as the gangly pup galloped toward him. He glanced around. "Is someone with you?" He bent down, and Bentley bounded into his arms.

Bentley wagged his thick whip of a tail. He strained his neck to try to lick Charles's face.

I'm so glad I found you! I thought I could smell you on this trail. I smell trouble, too. Does somebody need my help?

"Hello?" Charles called out. "Is anyone there?"

His parents and Bruce joined in. "Hello!" Dad shouted, cupping his hands around his mouth. "Did someone bring Bentley? Helloooo!" There was no response, just a happy yip from the puppy with the big paws and the slate-blue eyes.

"Lizzie said Weimaraners are good tracking dogs!" Charles said. "Maybe we can get him to help us find Buddy."

"Give him something of Buddy's," Bruce advised, "so he can get the scent."

Buddy had run off with his leash, so they needed to find something else.

Dad searched his backpack. "I have an old leash in here, but it probably doesn't smell like Buddy. It's one we use for foster dogs," he said, pulling out a black leash.

Charles took it and snapped the leash onto Bentley's collar so he couldn't run off. They didn't need two lost dogs on their hands.

"I can't find anything with Buddy's scent," Dad said when he got to the bottom of his pack.

"Oh! He slept on my fleece last night," Charles said. Quickly, he unzipped his jacket and pulled his arms out of the sleeves. "Here, Bentley. Smell this." Charles knelt down and held the blue fleece to Bentley's nose. He could see some of Buddy's short brown hairs caught in the nubby material.

Bentley buried his wet, brown nose in the fleece, his tail still wagging.

I know that smell. It's my friend! Where is my friend?

"See?" Charles said to the puppy. "It smells like Buddy. Buddy's lost. You need to help us find him."

Bentley began to whimper. The puppy pushed his nose back into the jacket, then looked up and glanced around. Charles held his breath. Bentley looked first at Mom, then Dad, and then Charles. He took a deep breath.

Then he sneezed.

Charles's shoulders drooped. He had thought Bentley understood.

Bentley let out a bark and wagged his tail.

What are we waiting for? Let's go find my friend!

The silver pup trotted off up the trail, the leash dragging behind him. He barked again.

"Grab his leash!" Mom yelled.

Charles jumped forward and stepped on the leash, then bent to take hold of it. "Got him!" he said. "Let's go, Bentley!"

Bentley lowered his nose to the ground. He took a couple of sniffs and a couple of steps. He moved quickly. *Sniff, sniff. Step, step. Sniff, sniff. Step, step.* He'd stop and smell the air, his nose pointed up to the sky. His nose was always working, and so were his legs. He tugged on the leash, leading Charles uphill, off the trail. Charles struggled to keep pace, slipping on wet clumps of leaves and loose rocks.

"I think I hear water!" he yelled out. He remembered that the Greenies were hiking on the waterfall trail that day. Lizzie had said it was one of the hardest.

"I just got a message," Bruce said, holding up his walkie-talkie. "Buddy isn't with the nature group. But they're looking for him." He paused.

"I also got a message from Melvin Merrick. He just realized that Bentley was missing, too. I guess he figured out how to get loose."

Charles wasn't surprised. Bentley was smart. He had probably learned how to open the latch on his crate. Charles wondered if Bentley had sensed something was wrong. He sure seemed to want to help. The puppy stuck his nose in the dirt again and whined. Charles had the feeling he smelled Buddy.

"Should we take Bentley back?" Mom asked. "I don't want Mr. Merrick to worry."

"No!" Charles said. He held on to the leash as Bentley tugged him uphill. "He's getting close. I know he is."

Bruce nodded. "Melvin knows that Bentley is safe with us," the ranger said. "Also, Melvin said he's sending someone. Someone who can help."

CHAPTER TEN

"Hey, down there!"

Everyone looked up to see who was yelling. It was Lizzie!

"We heard there's a puppy missing. We're searching for it," Lizzie called from a path above them. Charles tilted his head way back to see her waving from the top of a steep hill.

"Lizzie," Dad called back, using his calm firefighter voice. "The missing puppy is Buddy. Don't worry. We think we're close to finding him."

"What can we do?" Now Charles could see Maria standing next to Lizzie.

"Can you search up there?" Dad asked. "We think Buddy may have been trying to find you."

"Of course," Lizzie said. She sounded confident. Charles knew that Lizzie liked to have a job.

"He still has on his red leash!" Charles yelled up to her.

The forest began to echo with calls for Buddy. Bentley ignored the noise and kept his nose to the ground, smelling everything. He spent a long time sniffing a big rock with shiny flecks in it, and then he moved on. Then, at the bottom of a steep, muddy hill, Bentley stopped. He cocked his head to one side. He lifted one of his floppy ears. He sniffed the air. He barked.

I hear something. I smell something, too. It smells like our friend.

"What is it, Bentley?" Charles asked. With everyone yelling Buddy's name, it was hard to hear anything else. He strained his ears. Then he heard a tiny whine from above. "Buddy?" Charles cried. "Buddy! Where are you?"

Charles stared up the steep hill. "Buddy?" he yelled again. Bentley began to scramble up the hill. He found a rocky ledge and jumped up onto it, smelling the soggy brown leaves some more.

"Buddy!" Charles couldn't wait any longer. He grabbed a sapling and tried to pull himself up. The thin trunk of the tiny tree bent in his hand.

"Hold on! Hold on!" someone called. "That's not safe! It's too wet."

Charles turned around. A man was running toward them. Charles didn't know him, but he looked familiar.

"Holling!" Bruce called out. "You all, this is Holling. He's Melvin's boy."

Holling did not look like a boy. He was a man. He was probably close to Logan's age, but he was taller. He also had a short, tidy beard like his dad, Mr. Merrick.

"You still looking for your dog?" Holling asked.

"Yes," Charles said. "Bentley has been tracking him. We think he's up this hill."

Holling looked up and whistled. "Hill? I'd say it's more like a cliff," he said. "I'm not sure how your pup got up there, but I think Bentley is right."

Holling walked over to give Bentley a scratch between the ears. "Did you get us close, boy?" he asked. Bentley began wagging his tail so hard his whole body swayed back and forth. "How did you know these folks needed you? Did you let yourself out so you could help them?" he asked. "My dad will be glad you're okay." Bentley rested his chin in Holling's open hand and whimpered a little. "Dad was right when he told me about you. He said you're one sweet pup."

Do I know you? I feel like I know you.

Holling studied the ridge.

"Holling used to lead a tracking hike at Misty Valley," Bruce told the Petersons. "He's an expert on following trails."

"Well, maybe not an expert," said Holling. "But I know a little. We'd try to follow an animal's path by looking for clues," he explained. "I run a similar hike at the camp where I work now."

He walked closer to the ridge. "Some animal definitely came this way. You can see where its paws dug into the wet earth." He pointed to where the leaves were overturned. "And up there, that fern has broken fronds." He pointed to a ledge farther up. He paused, peering at the ground. "And was something dragging behind him? There's a trail in the leaves."

"Yes," Dad said. "Buddy still had his leash on."

Charles stared at Holling. He wasn't at all what Charles had expected. He didn't wear a suit, and he probably didn't drive a fancy car, either. Plus, he was like a wildlife detective, which was totally cool. Charles was learning so much from him. Even Lizzie didn't know this stuff, with all her camping. Charles noticed how Bentley leaned up against Holling's knee. The pup sure seemed to like Holling. If only Holling wasn't so against getting another dog!

Just then, they all heard a clear, sad whine.

"Buddy!" Charles yelled.

Bentley barked. He caught Charles off guard and yanked the leash from his hand. The puppy bolted up the hill.

"Whoa!" Holling watched Bentley. "I'm coming after you, little guy." Holling stood back to examine the ridge. Then, with a big stretch, he stepped up to a mossy ledge. He grabbed the base of a young tree and pulled himself farther.

"I see the leash!" It was Lizzie. She and Maria were leaning over a wood railing at the top of the trail. Lizzie pointed. "Bentley found it, but I still can't see Buddy."

"On my way!" Holling called out.

He sounded calm and sure of himself—*the same way Dad sounds in an emergency*, thought Charles.

Charles backed up to watch Holling's every move. Bentley watched him from above. The puppy followed Holling with his keen, blue-gray eyes. He barked.

I found my friend! I tracked him all the way up here. Hurry! You can help!

Step by step, Holling made his way up the dirt-and-rock wall. He was moving fast—maybe too fast. Charles gasped when he saw Holling's boot slip.

Charles held his breath. Holling hung on to a ledge, his feet dangling in the air. He swung his body sideways to land his foot on the edge of a flat rock. Then he pulled himself up to the next level, where the hill was less steep. Clumps of wet earth fell to the ground as he climbed almost all the way to the top. "I see your dog!" he yelled, between raspy breaths. "He's all right! His leash was caught between two rocks."

Charles watched, still holding his breath. When Holling caught up with Bentley, the pup greeted Holling with happy barks. Holling pet him, and Bentley licked his hands. "Good boy. Good boy, Bentley." Then Holling bent down to pick up Buddy. He gave him a hug. "Here we come," he said as he worked the rest of the way up the hill, carrying Buddy under his arm. At the top, he ducked under the fence.

Lizzie and Maria were there to meet them. Charles rushed back to the trail. It would only take a few moments to run up the easier way. He couldn't wait to hug Buddy, too!

Maria and the Petersons made a big fuss over Buddy.

Meanwhile, Holling and Bruce gave Bentley lots of love. "He did a fine job tracking that puppy," Bruce said. "Especially when you figure he's still only a puppy himself."

"My dad sure thinks a lot of him," Holling said. He held Bentley in his arms and rubbed his soft puppy belly. "I didn't think he'd ever care for a dog the way he cared for Bones."

"That's what he said about you!" Charles exclaimed. "He said you'd never get another dog after Bones, that you loved Bones too much."

Holling smiled. "You can never love a dog *too* much," he said. "I guess I claimed I would never get another dog. I probably meant it at the time. But a person can change his mind, can't he?"

Maybe Holling wanted to adopt Bentley! Charles quickly went through the checklist in his mind. What were all the things Bentley needed for a good home? It was hard to remember. He wanted to ask the big question, but he suddenly felt a little shy about it. He looked over at Lizzie. She was never shy. If he didn't ask now, she'd probably jump in and do it. She might be a big-time camper now, but he was the one who had figured out the best home for Bentley. He might as well finish what he'd started.

Charles cleared his throat. "Um," he said, "do you think you might want to adopt Bentley?"

"I think he might have already adopted me," Holling said, laughing as the puppy licked his face.

Charles thought they seemed perfect together. They both liked the outdoors. Holling was outside all the time; he didn't have to stay behind a reception desk like his dad. Holling and Bentley were both athletic and fun.

"But what about winter?" Charles asked. "Don't you go to the cold ski resorts, with Logan?"

"Not anymore," Holling said. "My camp is busy all year, so I don't go up north. We do have cross-country skiing if it snows enough."

Charles glanced over at Lizzie with a question in his eyes. She nodded. Charles nodded back.

Later, Charles remembered one more thing that was on his checklist. The Petersons were all packed up. They stood in the parking lot, getting ready to leave. Mr. Merrick, Holling, and Bentley had just come out to say good-bye. That's when Charles remembered. "Kids!" Charles blurted out. Everyone looked at him. "I forgot to ask if you have kids! Bentley likes kids, and he'd love having a whole family to keep him company."

Holling laughed. "I forgot to say that my kids will be the most excited of all," Holling admitted. "I just called them, and they can't wait to meet this sweet guy. The campers will love him, too."

"My grandkids have been asking for a dog forever," Mr. Merrick said. "Charles, I'm not sure how you changed Holling's mind, but thank you. I was hoping Bentley could stay in the family."

Bentley and Buddy were saying their good-byes, too. Buddy was on his back with his paws in the air. Bentley stood over him, wagging his tail.

"I didn't do anything," Charles said to Mr. Merrick. "It was all Bentley."

It was true, Charles thought. Bentley made it happen. Because Bentley knew something was wrong, he'd escaped from his crate. Because Bentley escaped from his crate, he was able to track Buddy. Because Bentley tracked Buddy, Holling had the chance to see what a great dog Bentley really was. And seeing that made Holling realize that he was ready to have a dog again — and that Bentley was the dog he wanted. In the end, Bentley knew just what he needed to do to get a new forever family. Charles smiled. Maybe some Weimaraners really were smarter than their owners. Maybe Bentley was smarter than them all!

PUPPY TIPS

Camping with your dog can be a whole lot of fun. Hiking in the woods, swimming in rivers or lakes, sleeping in a tent—what a special adventure to share with your favorite pal! It's important to keep your dog safe when you're in the wilderness. Make sure you have all his or her supplies: food, water, dishes, a nice soft bed. Your dog should be wearing a collar with tags that show your address and phone number, and you should have a good sturdy leash and harness for hiking. And don't forget to register your dog the way Charles and his dad registered Buddy, so that campground officials know that your pet is with you. Have fun, and don't forget to share a hot dog with your favorite buddy!

Dear Reader,

Misty Valley, the camp I made up for this book, seems like it would be such a fun place to be! I'm not sure I would dare to do the Flying Squirrel, but I would enjoy the hiking and birdwatching. I love being in nature anytime, especially with a dog.

I never went to summer camp, but I did go to dog camp a few times with my dog Django. We spent our days with lots of other dogs and dog owners, and tried out all sorts of activities from tracking to agility to costume contests. He loved it and so did I. Django died of old age a few years ago, but I'll always treasure the memories of our time at camp.

Yours from the Puppy Place,

Ellen Miles

ABOUT THE AUTHOR

Ellen Miles loves dogs, which is why she has a great time writing the Puppy Place books. And guess what? She loves cats, too! (In fact, her very first pet was a beautiful tortoiseshell cat named Jenny.) That's why she came up with the Kitty Corner series. Ellen lives in Vermont and loves to be outdoors with her dog, Zipper, every day, walking, biking, skiing, or swimming, depending on the season. She also loves to read, cook, explore her beautiful state, play with dogs, and hang out with friends and family.

Visit Ellen at ellenmiles.net.